D0050759

Here are some other Edge Books
from Henry Holt you will enjoy:

A Way Out of No Way
Writings About Growing Up Black in America
edited by Jacqueline Woodson

American Eyes
New Asian-American Short Stories for Young Adults
edited by Lori M. Carlson

Barrio Streets Carnival Dreams
Three Generations of Latino Artistry
edited by Lori M. Carlson

The Beautiful Days of My Youth
My Six Months in Auschwitz and Plaszow
by Ana Novac
translated from the French by George Newman

Cool Salsa
Bilingual Poems on Growing Up Latino in the United States
edited by Lori M. Carlson

Damned Strong Love
The True Story of Willi G. and Stefan K.
by Lutz van Dijk
translated from the German by Elizabeth D. Crawford

Hit the Nerve
New Voices of the American Theater
edited by Stephen Vincent Brennan

The Long Season of Rain
by Helen Kim

One Bird
by Kyoko Mori

Shizuko's Daughter
by Kyoko Mori

We're Alive and Life Goes On
A Theresienstadt Diary
by Eva Roubíčková
translated from the German by Zaia Alexander

We are Witnesses
The Diaries of Five Teenagers Who Died in the Holocaust
by Jacob Boas

Earth-Shattering Poems

Earth-Shattering Poems

Edited by
Liz Rosenberg

HENRY HOLT AND COMPANY
NEW YORK

Henry Holt and Company, Inc.
Publishers since 1866
115 West 18th Street
New York, New York 10011

Henry Holt is a registered
trademark of Henry Holt and Company, Inc.

Published in Canada by Fitzhenry & Whiteside Ltd.,
195 Allstate Parkway, Markham, Ontario L3R 4T8.

Library of Congress Cataloging-in-Publication Data

Earth-shattering poems / edited by Liz Rosenberg.
     p.   cm.
   Summary: A collection of poems that capture intense experiences
and emotions by such authors as Sappho, John Keats, Emily Dickinson,
Pablo Neruda, Sharon Olds, and J. E. Wei.
    1. Young adult poetry.   [1. Poetry—Collections.]   I. Rosenberg, Liz.
PN6109.97.E28   1997   808.81—dc21   97-16097

ISBN 0-8050-4821-9

First Edition—1998

Printed in the United States of America on acid-free paper.∞

Book design by Debbie Glasserman

10 9 8 7 6 5 4 3 2 1

CONTENTS

This book is dedicated to two of my favorite teenagers, my nieces, Vanessa and Becca; and to my nephews, Josh, no longer a teenager, and Adam, a preteen; and, of course, to their cousin, the almost-double-digit great and amazing Eli.

With thanks to my calm and faithful editor, Marc Aronson, and to his assistant, Matt Rosen, who has done so many things, great and small, on behalf of this book; and to the Comparative Literature Department at Binghamton University, and to the creative writing program, where I teach.

And finally: in memory of Constance Coiner and twelve-year-old Ana Duarte-Coiner, killed on TWA flight 800 to Paris—even in the face of their earth-shattering absence, shining lights always.

INTRODUCTION

This is a book of poems for young people. I was thinking of readers from roughly age twelve to twenty, but my nine-year-old son loved many of these poems, and so did his twenty-three-year-old sitter. Poetry is ageless; we each step into it at the right moment for us. No one can enforce poetry; if no one would try, more people might realize they want and need it. It's around us all the time, of course—for instance, in the form of song lyrics. I don't know any group of people more intensely responsive to songs than twelve- to twenty-year-olds. And if you bother to listen to the lyrics, you'll find that they can be rough, mysterious, sexy, nonsensical, depressing, dangerous, contradictory, hard to decode—all the things people say they dislike about poetry.

This book contains poetry in its purest, or most stripped-down, form: without benefit of melody or instrumentation or even the spoken voice (unless you say the poems aloud, which is always a good idea). I believe that all great poetry has its own kind of music, its own rhythm, but I'm not going to try to argue persuasively on poetry's behalf. I would say that it is all right to be partly confused by a poem; it's all right if you can only grab hold of one corner of it, because eventually that corner may be enough to pull you all the way through. Sometimes we love poetry because we *don't* completely understand it. Like a well-made garden, it has mystery or, as one of the poets here, Greg Moglia, describes it, "infinite renewal." One of my students once said, "Good poetry is like a top. It spins away from you at the end, and keeps on going." That is very different from, say, William Butler Yeats's idea that poetry is a perfectly made object that clicks "shut like a box." But there has to be some point of entrance, too. Like a great song or, really, any work of art, it either hits you or it doesn't.

People often turn to poetry in peak moments—moments of extreme joy, or sorrow, or confusion. Here again, it seems to me that poetry and adolescence make a perfect pair. Many teenagers write poetry, sometimes for the first and only time in their lives. It is a form dedicated to intensity. In this book, I've deliberately chosen poems that speak *most* powerfully to our most intense experiences and emotions—hence the title, *Earth-Shattering Poems*. That's how these poems struck me, often over the course of a number of years. How can I justify such a term? To me, "The Song of Wandering Aengus" is earth-shatteringly beautiful; "If You Forget Me," earth-shatteringly romantic; "Her Husband Asks Her to Buy a Bolt of Silk," earth-shatteringly scathing. These are all poems that shook me, and the aftershocks continue for a lifetime.

Many people have tried to describe how great poetry affects them. The poet W. H. Auden claimed it made his beard prickle so it was easy to shave. Emily Dickinson, a poet included here, once said, "If I read a book and it makes my whole body so cold no fire can ever warm me, I know that is poetry. If I feel physically as if the top of my head were taken off, I know that is poetry. These are the only ways I know it. Is there any other way?" There are probably as many responses to poetry as there are responders.

But there are other meanings, for me, to the phrase "earth-shattering poetry." Something in these poems shatters my sense both of time and place. Sappho's speechlessness in the face of the one she adores is as fresh, coming from a small Greek island in the Aegean Sea twenty-five hundred years ago, as Kate Schmitt, the youngest poet here, describing how she feels when she says goodbye to someone she loves.

The poems here are organized chronologically by the birthdate of the poet. These poems detonate from all over the globe—from ancient China and Persia to Spain during the Spanish Civil War to Russia during the Stalinist terrors to Germany, France, Britain, Japan, El Salvador, Peru, and America today. Many of them appear here in translation, and so, inevitably, some of the original word-music is lost or changed. One can return to the original—sometimes even with the most basic high-school French or Spanish, for instance—and gain a deeper understanding of the poem just by hearing how the original sounds reverberate in the mouth and ears. (Imagine setting your favorite song to some other music. Now imagine hearing the original music for the first time.) If for no other reason—and there are so many—I'd say that every poet, and every reader of poetry, ought to try translating poetry at least once.

For every poem that appears here, there are thousands more—oceans of African poems and stories, Native American chants, Eskimo poems, Australian aboriginal songs. (See Naomi Shahib Nye's panoramic collection *This Same Sky: Poems from Around the World*.) I could only include a sampling of what I know and love best. Some of these poems are very dark. Others break open with joy. Sometimes they seem to speak to each other over vast spaces of time and place. Their cries of laughter or pain rise up all over the earth.

There is a belief in ancient Hebrew texts that we were all once part of God, but that we somehow broke and scattered from that divine source. Perhaps these poems are the result of some such shattering. They are some of the ways we talk to ourselves in the dark, comfort ourselves after a death, boast in the face of danger, remember the dead, proclaim our love, weep, and express our passion, rage, confusion, or ecstasy. This is what lives in these poems. And they are only a fraction of what is out there. I hope they will lead readers to find more.

Earth-Shattering Poems

FRAGMENT

sappho (620–550 B.C.)

He seems to me like a god,
that man, who sits closely
facing you
and hears you sweetly speaking,

laughing, reeking with that desire
which fluttered the heart in my chest.
For when I see you suddenly
my voice deserts me.

My tongue lies broken in my mouth, unable to move.
Fire races under my skin.
My eyes see nothing,
in my ears, only drumming thunder.

The sweat pours down, trembling
seizes me, I turn greener than grass;
at such times I feel my death
draw near.

translated from the Greek by Saul Levin and Liz Rosenberg

HER HUSBAND ASKS HER TO BUY A BOLT OF SILK

ch'en t'ao (eleventh century)

The wind is cruel. Her clothes are worn and thin.
The weaver girl blows on her fingers.
Beside the dark window, back and forth,
She throws a shuttle like a lump of ice.
During the short Winter day
She can scarcely weave one foot of brocade.
And you expect me to make a folk song of this,
For your silken girls to sing?

translated from the Chinese by Kenneth Rexroth

ACROSS THE DOORSILL

rumi (1207–1273)

The breeze at dawn has secrets to tell you. Don't go back to
   sleep!
You must ask for what you really want. Don't go back to
   sleep!
People are going back and forth across the doorsill where
                              the two worlds touch.
The door is round and open. Don't go back to sleep!

translated from the Persian by Coleman Barks

THE WAY OF LOVE

rumi

The way of love is not
a subtle argument.

The door there
is devastation.

Birds make great sky-circles
of their freedom.
How do they learn it?

They fall, and falling,
they're given wings.

translated from the Persian by Coleman Barks

HAIKU

basho (1664–1694)

Old pond
Frog plunks in
—water's sound

translated from the Japanese by Liz Rosenberg

LONDON

william blake (1757–1827)

I wander thro' each charter'd street,
Near where the charter'd Thames does flow
And mark in every face I meet
Marks of weakness, marks of woe.

In every cry of every Man,
In every Infants cry of fear,
In every voice; in every ban,
The mind-forg'd manacles I hear

How the Chimney-sweepers cry
Every blackning Church appalls,
And the hapless Soldiers sigh
Runs in blood down Palace walls

But most thro' midnight streets I hear
How the youthful Harlots curse
Blasts the new-born Infants tear
And blights with plagues the Marriage hearse.

A POISON TREE

william blake

I was angry with my friend:
I told my wrath, my wrath did end.
I was angry with my foe:
I told it not, my wrath did grow.

And I waterd it in fears,
Night & morning with my tears:
And I sunned it with smiles,
And with soft deceitful wiles.

And it grew both day and night,
Till it bore an apple bright.
And my foe beheld it shine,
And he knew that it was mine.

And into my garden stole,
When the night had veild the pole;
In the morning glad I see,
My foe outstretchd beneath the tree.

THE SICK ROSE

william blake

O Rose thou art sick.
The invisible worm,
That flies in the night
In the howling storm:

Has found out thy bed
Of crimson joy:
And his dark secret love
Does thy life destroy.

THIS WORLD OF DEW

issa (1763–1827)

This world of dew
is only a world of dew
—And yet . . .

translated from the Japanese by Liz Rosenberg

friedrich hölderlin (1770–1843)

Elysium
    Yes there at last I find
       Near you, the gods of death
    Diotima there   and heroes.

I'd sing of you
    But only tears.
   And in the night in which I wander extinguished from me
     is your
        Clear eye!
            Heavenly ghost

translated from the German by Liz Rosenberg

THE WHOLE WORLD

hebrew folk song
(rabbi nachman of bratzlav, 1772–1811)

The whole world is a very narrow bridge
but the most important thing is not to be afraid at all.

translated from the Yiddish by Liz Rosenberg

BRIGHT STAR

john keats (1795–1821)

Bright star, would I were steadfast as thou art—
  Not in lone splendor hung aloft the night
And watching, with eternal lids apart,
  Like nature's patient, sleepless Eremite,
The moving waters at their priestlike task
  Of pure ablution round earth's human shores,
Or gazing on the new soft fallen mask
  Of snow upon the mountains and the moors—
No—yet still steadfast, still unchangeable,
  Pillowed upon my fair love's ripening breast,
To feel forever its soft fall and swell,
  Awake forever in a sweet unrest,
Still, still to hear her tender-taken breath,
And so live ever—or else swoon to death.

THIS LIVING HAND

john keats

This living hand, now warm and capable
Of earnest grasping, would, if it were cold
And in the icy silence of the tomb,
So haunt thy days and chill thy dreaming nights
That thou wouldst wish thine own heart dry of blood
So in my veins red life might stream again,
And thou be conscience-calmed—see here it is—
I hold it towards you.

from IN MEMORIAM A. H. H.

alfred, lord tennyson (1809–1892)

7

Dark house, by which once more I stand
    Here in the long unlovely street,
    Doors, where my heart was used to beat
So quickly, waiting for a hand,

A hand that can be clasp'd no more —
    Behold me, for I cannot sleep,
    And like a guilty thing I creep
At earliest morning to the door.

He is not here; but far away
    The noise of life begins again,
    And ghastly thro' the drizzling rain
On the bald street breaks the blank day.

LOOK DOWN FAIR MOON

walt whitman (1819–1892)

Look down fair moon and bathe this scene,
Pour softly down night's nimbus floods on faces ghastly,
    swollen, purple,
On the dead on their backs with arms toss'd wide,
Pour down your unstinted nimbus sacred moon.

RECONCILIATION

walt whitman

Word over all, beautiful as the sky,
Beautiful that war and all its deeds of carnage must
    in time be utterly lost,
That the hands of the sisters Death and Night incessantly
    softly wash again, and ever again, this soil'd world;
For my enemy is dead, a man divine as myself is dead,
I look where he lies white-faced and still in the
    coffin—I draw near,
Bend down and touch lightly with my lips the white face
    in the coffin.

SOMETIMES WITH ONE I LOVE

walt whitman

Sometimes with one I love I fill myself with rage for
    fear I effuse unreturn'd love,
But now I think there is no unreturn'd love, the pay is
    certain one way or another,
(I loved a certain person ardently and my love was
    not return'd,
Yet out of that I have written these songs.)

GET DRUNK!

charles baudelaire (1821–1867)

One must always be drunk. That's it; the only question. So as not to feel the hideous weight of Time breaking your shoulders and bowing you to the earth, one must be drunk without rest.

On what? On wine, on poetry, or on virtue, as you please. But get drunk.

And if sometimes, on the steps of the palace, on the green grass of a ditch, in the gloomy solitude of your room, you wake—your drunkenness already ebbing or gone, ask the wind, the wave, the star; the bird, the clock, ask everything that flies, everything that moans or moves, everything that sings, everything that speaks, ask what time it is; and the wind, wave, star, bird, clock will tell you, "It's time to get drunk! So as not to be the martyred slaves of time, get drunk; get drunk without ceasing! On wine, on poetry, or on virtue, as you choose."

translated from the French by Liz Rosenberg

DOVER BEACH

matthew arnold (1822–1888)

The sea is calm to-night.
The tide is full, the moon lies fair
Upon the straits;—on the French coast, the light
Gleams, and is gone; the cliffs of England stand,
Glimmering and vast, out in the tranquil bay.
Come to the window, sweet is the night-air!
Only, from the lone line of spray
Where the sea meets the moon-blanch'd sand,
Listen! you hear the grating roar
Of pebbles which the waves draw back, and fling,
At their return, up the high strand,
Begin, and cease, and then again begin,
With tremulous cadence slow, and bring
The eternal note of sadness in.

Sophocles long ago
Heard it on the Ægæan, and it brought
Into his mind the turbid ebb and flow
Of human misery; we
Find also in the sound a thought,
Hearing it by this distant northern sea.

The Sea of Faith
Was once, too, at the full, and round earth's shore

Lay like the folds of a bright girdle furl'd.
But now I only hear
Its melancholy, long, withdrawing roar,
Retreating, to the breath
Of the night-wind down the vast edges drear
And naked shingles of the world.

Ah, love, let us be true
To one another! for the world, which seems
To lie before us like a land of dreams,
So various, so beautiful, so new,
Hath really neither joy, nor love, nor light,
Nor certitude, nor peace, nor help for pain;
And we are here as on a darkling plain
Swept with confused alarms of struggle and flight,
Where ignorant armies clash by night.

WILD NIGHTS

emily dickinson (1830–1886)

Wild Nights—Wild Nights!
Were I with thee
Wild Nights should be
Our luxury!

Futile—the Winds—
To a Heart in port—
Done with the Compass—
Done with the Chart!

Rowing in Eden—
Ah, the Sea!
Might I but moor—Tonight—
In Thee!

THE SONG OF WANDERING AENGUS

william butler yeats (1865-1939)

I went out to the hazel wood,
Because a fire was in my head,
And cut and peeled a hazel wand,
And hooked a berry to a thread;
And when white moths were on the wing,
And moth-like stars were flickering out,
I dropped the berry in a stream
And caught a little silver trout.

When I had laid it on the floor
I went to blow the fire a-flame,
But something rustled on the floor,
And someone called me by my name:
It had become a glimmering girl
With apple blossom in her hair
Who called me by my name and ran
And faded through the brightening air.

Though I am old with wandering
Through hollow lands and hilly lands,
I will find out where she has gone,

And kiss her lips and take her hands;
And walk among long dappled grass,
And pluck till time and times are done
The silver apples of the moon,
The golden apples of the sun.

WHEN YOU ARE OLD

william butler yeats

When you are old and gray and full of sleep,
And nodding by the fire, take down this book,
And slowly read, and dream of the soft look
Your eyes once had, and of their shadows deep;
How many loved your moments of glad grace,
And loved your beauty with love false or true;
But one man loved the pilgrim soul in you,
And loved the sorrows of your changing face.

And bending down beside the glowing bars
Murmur, a little sadly, how love fled
And paced upon the mountains overhead
And hid his face amid a crowd of stars.

ARCHAIC TORSO OF APOLLO

rainer maria rilke (1875-1926)

We have no idea what his fantastic head
was like, where the eyeballs were slowly swelling. But
his body now is glowing like a gas lamp,
whose inner eyes, only turned down a little,

hold their flame, shine. If there weren't light, the curve
of the breast wouldn't blind you, and in the swerve
of the thighs a smile wouldn't keep on going
toward the place where the seeds are.

If there weren't light, this stone would look cut off
where it drops clearly from the shoulders,
its skin wouldn't gleam like the fur of a wild animal,

and the body wouldn't send out light from every edge
as a star does . . . for there is no place at all
that isn't looking at you. You must change your life.

translated from the German by Robert Bly

THREE SPANISH FOLK SONGS

I

On the day you were born,
bells rang,
graves opened,
and the dead arose.

II

—What have you eaten
that's made you so pale?
I've eaten the ashes
of love's fire.

III

When they brought me the news
that you don't love me,
I didn't drown myself in the sea . . .
The water was too cold.

translated from the Russian by Martin Bidney

IN A STATION OF THE METRO

ezra pound (1885–1972)

The apparition of these faces in the crowd;
Petals on a wet, black bough.

from REQUIEM

anna akhmatova (1889–1966)

No, not under a foreign heavenly-cope, and
Not canopied by foreign wings—
I was with my people in those hours,
There where, unhappily, my people were.

In the fearful years of the Yezhov terror I spent seventeen
months in prison queues in Leningrad. One day somebody
'identified' me. Beside me, in the queue, there was a woman
with blue lips. She had, of course, never heard of me; but she
suddenly came out of that trance so common to us all and
whispered in my ear (everybody spoke in whispers there):
'Can you describe this?' And I said: 'Yes, I can.' And then
something like the shadow of a smile crossed what had once
been her face.

1 APRIL 1957, LENINGRAD

EPILOGUE

I

There I learned how faces fall apart,
How fear looks out from under the eyelids,
How deep are the hieroglyphics

Cut by suffering on people's cheeks.
There I learned how silver can inherit
The black, the ash-blond, overnight,
The smiles that faded from the poor in spirit,
Terror's dry coughing sound.
And I pray not only for myself,
But also for all those who stood there
In bitter cold, or in the July heat,
Under that red blind prison-wall.

I I

Again the hands of the clock are nearing
The unforgettable hour. I see, hear, touch

All of you: the cripple they had to support
Painfully to the end of the line; the moribund;

And the girl who would shake her beautiful
      head and
Say: 'I come here as if it were home.'

I should like to call you all by name,
But they have lost the lists. . . .

I have woven for them a great shroud
Out of the poor words I overheard them speak.

I remember them always and everywhere,
And if they shut my tormented mouth,

Through which a hundred million of my people cry,
Let them remember me also. . . .

And if ever in this country they should want
To build me a monument

I consent to that honour,
But only on condition that they

Erect it not on the sea-shore where I was born:
My last links there were broken long ago,

Nor by the stump in the Royal Gardens,
Where an inconsolable young shade is seeking me,

But here, where I stood for three hundred hours
And where they never, never opened the doors for me.

Lest in blessed death I should forget
The grinding scream of the Black Marias,

The hideous clanging gate, the old
Woman wailing like a wounded beast.

And may the melting snow drop like tears
From my motionless bronze eyelids,

And the prison pigeons coo above me
And the ships sail slowly down the Neva.

translated from the Russian by D. M. Thomas

anna akhmatova

I did not lock the door
I didn't light the candles.
You don't know how, tired as I was,
I didn't dare go to sleep.

To watch the streaks of light dying
in the twilight dark of the pines.
I am getting drunk on the sound
of a voice like yours in the hall.

And to know that everything is lost,
that life — is a cursed hell.
O, I was so certain
you would come back.

translated from the Russian by Liz Rosenberg and Nadia Zarembo

In early summer, Russia experiences nearly twenty-four hours of light a day, a time period called a "white night." "White night" is also an expression used to describe insomnia, a condition in which one doesn't sleep at all. With this poem, as it happens, both meanings are correct.

THE BLACK RIDERS

césar vallejo (1892–1938)

There are blows in life so violent — I can't answer!
Blows as if from the hatred of God; as if before them,
the deep waters of everything lived through
were backed up in the soul . . . I can't answer!

Not many; but they exist . . . They open dark ravines
in the most ferocious face and in the most bull-like back.
Perhaps they are the horses of that heathen Attila,
or the black riders sent to us by Death.

They are the slips backward made by the Christs of the soul,
away from some holy faith that is sneered at by Events.
These blows that are bloody are the crackling sounds
from some bread that burns at the oven door.

And man . . . poor man! . . . poor man! He swings his eyes, as
when a man behind us calls us by clapping his hands;
swings his crazy eyes, and everything alive
is backed up, like a pool of guilt, in that glance.

There are blows in life so violent . . . I can't answer!

translated from the Spanish by Robert Bly

LAMENT FOR IGNACIO SÁNCHEZ MEJÍAS

federico garcía lorca (1898–1936)

1. THE GORING AND THE DEATH

At five in the afternoon.
It was exactly five in the afternoon.
A boy brought the white sheet
at five in the afternoon.
A basketful of lime in readiness
at five in the afternoon.
Beyond that, death and death alone
at five in the afternoon.

The wind carried off wisps of cotton
at five in the afternoon.
And oxide dispersed glass and nickel
at five in the afternoon.
Dove locked in struggle with leopard
at five in the afternoon.
A thigh with a horn of desolation
at five in the afternoon.
The bass strings began to throb
at five in the afternoon.
The bells of arsenic, the smoke
at five in the afternoon.

At street corners silence clustering
at five in the afternoon.
Only the bull with upbeat heart
at five in the afternoon.
When snow-cold sweat began to form
at five in the afternoon,
when iodine had overspread the ring
at five in the afternoon,
death laid eggs in the wound
at five in the afternoon.
At five in the afternoon.
At exactly five in the afternoon.

A coffin on wheels is the bed
at five in the afternoon.
Bones and flutes resound in his ear
at five in the afternoon.
The bull was bellowing in his face
at five in the afternoon.
Death pangs turned the room iridescent
at five in the afternoon.
In the distance gangrene on the way
at five in the afternoon.
Lily-trumpet in the verdant groin
at five in the afternoon.
The wounds burned with the heat of suns
at five in the afternoon,
and the throng burst through the windows
at five in the afternoon.
At five in the afternoon.
Horrifying five in the afternoon!

The stroke of five on every clock.
The dark of five in the afternoon.

2. THE SPILLED BLOOD

No, I refuse to see it!

Tell the moon to come—
I refuse to see the blood
of Ignacio on the sand.

No, I refuse to see it!

The moon opened wide
trotting through quiet clouds
and the gray bullring of a dream
with willows at the palings.

No, I refuse to see it!
The remembering burns.
Send word to the jasmine
to bring its tiny whiteness.

No, I refuse to see it.

The cow of this ancient world
was running her dreary tongue
over snoutfuls of blood
spilled across the sand,
and the bulls of Guisando,
almost death and nearly stone,
lowed like two centuries

tired of treading earth.
No.
I refuse to see it!

Ignacio mounts the steps,
shouldering his full death.
He looked for daybreak
and daybreak there was none.
He seeks the clean line of his profile
and sleep leads him astray.
He looked for his shapely body
and found his gaping blood.
Don't tell me I have to see it.
I don't want to feel the spurts
slowly subsiding,
the gushes glistening
on the bleachers, spilling
on the corduroy and leather
of bloodthirsty masses.
Who shouts for me to come look?
Don't tell me I have to see it.

His eyes did not shut
when he saw the horns close in
but the terrible mothers
lifted their heads to watch.
And sweeping the herds of cattle
came an air of secret voices
called out to bulls of heaven
by pale ranchers of mist.

No prince ever was in Seville
that could even approach him,
no sword like his sword,
no heart so truly a heart.
Like a river of lions
the marvel of his strength,
and like a marble torso
the contour of his prudence.
An air of Rome's Andalusia
hung golden about his head,
while his laughter was as spikenard—
all intelligence and wit.
What a great fighter in the ring!
What a good mountaineer on the heights!
How gentle toward ears of grain!
How harsh applying the spurs!
How tender toward the dew!
How dazzling at the fair!
How magnificent when he wielded
the last banderillas of the dark.

But his sleep now is unending.
Now mosses and grass
pry open with practiced fingers
the flower of his skull.
And his blood now courses singing,
sings through salt marshes and meadows,
slides over stone-cold horns,
gropes soulless through the mist,
comes up against thousands of hooves

like some long, dark tongue of sadness,
to end in a pool gasping death
by the Guadalquivir of the stars.

Oh white wall of Spain!
Oh black bull of sorrow!
Oh hardened blood of Ignacio!
Oh nightingale of his veins!

No.
I refuse to see it!
There's no chalice to contain it,
no swallow to drink it up,
no glittering rime to chill it,
no chant, no outpouring of lilies,
no crystal to sheathe it in silver.
No.
I won't look at it, ever!

3. PRESENCE OF THE BODY

Stone is a forehead where dreams moan,
holding no curved water, no frozen cypress.
Stone is a shoulder meant to carry time,
with trees of tears and ribbons and planets.

I have watched gray rains running toward the waves,
lifting fragile, riddled arms
to avoid being snagged by outcrops of stone
which unknit their limbs without soaking in their blood.

Because stone gathers seeds and banks of cloud,
skeletons of larks, wolves dimming into shadow,
but yields no sound, no crystal, no fire—
yields only endless bullrings without walls.

Ignacio the wellborn lies here on stone.
He is finished. What has happened? See his face.
Death has overlaid him with pale sulphur
and given him a minotaur's dark head.

He is finished. Rain seeps through his mouth.
Air rushes frenzied from his sunken chest
and Love, wet to the bone with tears of snow,
warms himself among the highland herds.

What are they saying? Here rests fetid silence.
The body here before us hazes over.
The luminous form that once held nightingales
we now see being punctured through and through.

Who is rumpling the shroud? What he says is not so.
No one is singing here or weeping in silence,
spurring horses, frightening off snakes;
here all I want is wide-open eyes
to see that body that can never rest.

I want to see here the men with harsh voices.
Tamers of horses, subduers of rivers,
whose bones you hear straining, who sing
with mouths full of sunlight and flint.

I want to see them here. Here at the stone.
By this body with the severed reins.
I want them to show me a way out
for this captain shackled by death;

have them teach me to weep like a river,
a river of soft mists and steep banks,
that will bear Ignacio's body out of sight
and still the double snorting of the bull.

Out of sight to the round bullring of the crescent
moon that's like a bull stock-still with pain;
out of sight into the fishes' songless night
and into the white scrub of smoke congealed.

I don't want them covering his face with kerchiefs
to break him in to the wearing of death.
Go now, Ignacio. Feel no more the hot bellows.
Sleep, soar, repose. The sea dies too!

4. ABSENCE OF THE SOUL

The bull does not know you, nor the fig tree,
nor horses, nor the ants on your floors.
The child does not know you, nor the evening,
because your death is forever.

The saddleback of rock does not know you,
nor the black satin where you tore apart.

Your silent recollection does not know you
because your death is forever.

Autumn will return bringing snails,
misted-over grapes, and clustered mountains,
but none will wish to gaze in your eyes
because your death is forever.

Because your death is forever,
like everyone's who ever died on Earth,
like all dead bodies discarded
on rubbish heaps with mongrels' corpses.

No one knows you. No one. But I sing you—
sing your profile and your grace, for later on.
The signal ripeness of your mastery.
The way you sought death out, savored its taste.
The sadness just beneath your gay valor.

Not soon, if ever, will Andalusia see
so towering a man, so venturesome.
I sing his elegance with words that moan
and remember a sad breeze in the olive groves.

translated from the Spanish by Alan S. Trueblood

HARLEM

langston hughes (1902–1967)

What happens to a dream deferred?
   Does it dry up
   like a raisin in the sun?
   Or fester like a sore—
   And then run?
   Does it stink like rotten meat?
   Or crust and sugar over—
   like a syrupy sweet?

Maybe it just sags
   like a heavy load.

   Or does it explode?

IF YOU FORGET ME

pablo neruda (1904–1973)

I want you to know
one thing.

You know how this is:
if I look
at the crystal moon, at the red branch
of the slow autumn at my window,
if I touch
near the fire
the impalpable ash
or the wrinkled body of the log,
everything carries me to you,
as if everything that exists,
aromas, light, metals,
were little boats that sail
toward those isles of yours that wait for me.

Well, now,
if little by little you stop loving me
I shall stop loving you little by little.

If suddenly
you forget me
do not look for me,
for I shall already have forgotten you.

If you think it long and mad,
the wind of banners
that passes through my life,
and you decide
to leave me at the shore
of the heart where I have roots,
remember
that on that day,
at that hour,
I shall lift my arms
and my roots will set off
to seek another land.

But
if each day,
each hour,
you feel that you are destined for me
with implacable sweetness,
if each day a flower
climbs up to your lips to seek me,
ah my love, ah my own,
in me all that fire is repeated,
in me nothing is extinguished or forgotten,
my love feeds on your love, beloved,
and as long as you live it will be in your arms
without leaving mine.

translated from the Spanish by Donald D. Walsh

ENCOUNTER

czeslaw milosz (b. 1911)

We were riding through frozen fields in a wagon at dawn.
A red wing rose in the darkness.

And suddenly a hare ran across the road.
One of us pointed to it with his hand.

That was long ago. Today neither of them is alive,
Not the hare, not the man who made the gesture.

O my love, where are they, where are they going
The flash of a hand, streak of movement, rustle of pebbles.
I ask not out of sorrow, but in wonder.

translated from the Polish by Robert Hass and Czeslaw Milosz

THE POEM AS MASK

muriel rukeyser (1913–1980)

ORPHEUS

When I wrote of the women in their dances and wildness, it
    was a mask,
on their mountain, gold-hunting, singing, in orgy,
it was a mask; when I wrote of the god,
fragmented, exiled from himself, his life, the love gone
    down with song,
it was myself, split open, unable to speak, in exile from
    myself.

There is no mountain, there is no god, there is memory
of my torn life, myself split open in sleep, the rescued child
beside me among the doctors, and a word
of rescue from the great eyes.

No more masks! No more mythologies!

Now, for the first time, the god lifts his hand,
the fragments join in me with their own music.

MAN AND WIFE

robert lowell (1917–1978)

Tamed by *Miltown*, we lie on Mother's bed;
the rising sun in war paint dyes us red;
in broad daylight her gilded bed-posts shine,
abandoned, almost Dionysian.
At last the trees are green on Marlborough Street,
blossoms on our magnolia ignite
the morning with their murderous five days' white.
All night I've held your hand,
as if you had
a fourth time faced the kingdom of the mad—
its hackneyed speech, its homicidal eye—
and dragged me home alive. . . . Oh my *Petite*,
clearest of all God's creatures, still all air and nerve:
you were in your twenties, and I,
once hand on glass
and heart in mouth,
outdrank the Rahvs in the heat
of Greenwich Village, fainting at your feet—
too boiled and shy
and poker-faced to make a pass,
while the shrill verve
of your invective scorched the traditional South.

Now twelve years later, you turn your back.
Sleepless, you hold

your pillow to your hollows like a child;
your old-fashioned tirade—
loving, rapid, merciless—
breaks like the Atlantic Ocean on my head.

SKUNK HOUR

robert lowell

for Elizabeth Bishop

Nautilus Island's hermit
heiress still lives through winter in her Spartan cottage;
her sheep still graze above the sea.
Her son's a bishop. Her farmer
is first selectman in our village;
she's in her dotage.

Thirsting for
the hierarchic privacy
of Queen Victoria's century,
she buys up all
the eyesores facing her shore,
and lets them fall.

The season's ill—
we've lost our summer millionaire,
who seemed to leap from an L. L. Bean
catalogue. His nine-knot yawl
was auctioned off to lobstermen.
A red fox stain covers Blue Hill.

And now our fairy
decorator brightens his shop for fall;

his fishnet's filled with orange cork,
orange, his cobbler's bench and awl;
there is no money in his work,
he'd rather marry.

One dark night,
my Tudor Ford climbed the hill's skull;
I watched for love-cars. Lights turned down,
they lay together, hull to hull,
where the graveyard shelves on the town. . . .
My mind's not right.

A car radio bleats,
"Love, O careless Love. . . ." I hear
my ill-spirit sob in each blood cell,
as if my hand were at its throat. . . .
I myself am hell;
nobody's here—

only skunks, that search
in the moonlight for a bite to eat.
They march on their soles up Main Street:
white stripes, moonstruck eyes' red fire
under the chalk-dry and spar spire
of the Trinitarian Church.

I stand on top
of our back steps and breathe the rich air—

a mother skunk with her column of kittens swills the garbage
    pail.
She jabs her wedge-head in a cup
of sour cream, drops her ostrich tail,
and will not scare.

MARRIED

jack gilbert (b. 1926)

I came back from the funeral and crawled
around the apartment, crying hard,
searching for my wife's hair.
For two months got them from the drain,
from the vacuum cleaner, under the refrigerator,
and off the clothes in the closet.
But after other Japanese women came,
there was no way to be sure which were
hers, and I stopped. A year later,
repotting Michiko's avocado, I find
a long black hair tangled in the dirt.

LITTLE SLEEP'S-HEAD SPROUTING HAIR IN THE MOONLIGHT

galway kinnell (b. 1927)

1

You cry, waking from a nightmare.

When I sleepwalk
into your room, and pick you up,
and hold you up in the moonlight, you cling to me
hard,
as if clinging could save us. I think
you think
I will never die, I think I exude
to you the permanence of smoke or stars,
even as
my broken arms heal themselves around you.

2

I have heard you tell
the sun, *don't go down*, I have stood by
as you told the flower, *don't grow old*,
don't die. Little Maud,

I would blow the flame out of your silver cup,
I would suck the rot from your fingernail,
I would brush your sprouting hair of the dying light,
I would scrape the rust off your ivory bones,
I would help death escape through the little ribs of your
    body,
I would alchemize the ashes of your cradle back into wood,
I would let nothing of you go, ever,

until washerwomen
feel the clothes fall asleep in their hands,
and hens scratch their spell across hatchet blades,
and rats walk away from the cultures of the plague,
and iron twists weapons toward the true north,
and grease refuses to slide in the machinery of progress,
and men feel as free on earth as fleas on the bodies of men,
and lovers no longer whisper to the one beside them in the
    dark, O *corpse-to-be* . . .

And yet perhaps this is the reason you cry,
this the nightmare you wake crying from:
being forever
in the pre-trembling of a house that falls.

3

In a restaurant once, everyone
quietly eating, you clambered up
on my lap: to all

the mouthfuls rising toward
all the mouths, at the top of your voice
you cried
your one word, *caca! caca! caca!*
and each spoonful
stopped, a moment, in midair, in its withering
steam.

Yes,
you cling because
I, like you, only sooner
than you, will go down
the path of vanished alphabets,
the roadlessness
to the other side of the darkness,
your arms
like the shoes left behind,
like the adjectives in the halting speech
of very old men,
which used to be able to call up the forgotten nouns.

4

And you yourself,
some impossible Tuesday
in the year Two Thousand and Nine, will walk out
among the black stones
of the field, in the rain,
and the stones saying over their one word, *ci-gît, ci-gît, ci-gît,*

and the raindrops
hitting you on the fontanel
over and over, and you standing there
unable to let them in.

5

If one day it happens
you find yourself with someone you love
in a café at one end
of the Pont Mirabeau, at the zinc bar
where white wine stands in upward opening glasses,

and if you commit then, as we did, the error
of thinking,
one day all this will only be memory,

learn to reach deeper
into the sorrows
to come — to touch
the almost imaginary bones
under the face, to hear under the laughter
the wind crying across the stones. Kiss
the mouth
which tells you, *here,*
here is the world. This mouth. This laughter. These temple
    bones.

The still undanced cadence of vanishing.

6

In the light the moon
sends back, I can see in your eyes

the hand that waved once
in my father's eyes, a tiny kite
wobbling far up in the twilight of his last look,
and the angel
of all mortal things let go the string.

7

Back you go, into your crib.

The last blackbird lights up his gold wings: *farewell.*
Your eyes close inside your head,
in sleep. Already
in your dreams the hours begin to sing.

Little sleep's-head sprouting hair in the moonlight,
when I come back
we will go out together,
we will walk out together among
the ten thousand things,
each scratched in time with such knowledge, *the wages
of dying is love.*

LYING IN A HAMMOCK AT WILLIAM DUFFY'S FARM IN PINE ISLAND, MINNESOTA

james wright (1927–1980)

Over my head, I see the bronze butterfly,
Asleep on the black trunk,
Blowing like a leaf in green shadow.
Down the ravine behind the empty house,
The cowbells follow one another
Into the distances of the afternoon.
To my right,
In a field of sunlight between two pines,
The droppings of last year's horses
Blaze up into golden stones.
I lean back, as the evening darkens and comes on.
A chicken hawk floats over, looking for home.
I have wasted my life.

THE POEM OF CHALK

philip levine (b. 1928)

On the way to lower Broadway
this morning I faced a tall man
speaking to a piece of chalk
held in his right hand. The left
was open, and it kept the beat,
for his speech had a rhythm,
was a chant or dance, perhaps
even a poem in French, for he
was from Senegal and spoke French
so slowly and precisely that I
could understand as though
hurled back fifty years to my
high school classroom. A slender man,
elegant in his manner, neatly dressed
in the remnants of two blue suits,
his tie fixed squarely, his white shirt
spotless though unironed. He knew
the whole history of chalk, not only
of this particular piece, but also
the chalk with which I wrote
my name the day they welcomed
me back to school after the death
of my father. He knew feldspar,

he knew calcium, oyster shells, he
knew what creatures had given
their spines to become the dust time
pressed into these perfect cones,
he knew the sadness of classrooms
in December when the light fails
early and the words on the blackboard
abandon their grammar and sense
and then even their shapes so that
each letter points in every direction
at once and means nothing at all.
At first I thought his short beard
was frosted with chalk; as we stood
face to face, no more than a foot
apart, I saw the hairs were white,
for though youthful in his gestures
he was, like me, an aging man, though
far nobler in appearance with his high
carved cheekbones, his broad shoulders,
and clear dark eyes. He had the bearing
of a king of lower Broadway, someone
out of the mind of Shakespeare or
García Lorca, someone for whom loss
had sweetened into charity. We stood
for that one long minute, the two
of us sharing the final poem of chalk
while the great city raged around
us, and then the poem ended, as all
poems do, and his left hand dropped
to his side abruptly and he handed

me the piece of chalk. I bowed,
knowing how large a gift this was
and wrote my thanks on the air
where it might be heard forever
below the sea shell's stiffening cry.

LADY LAZARUS

sylvia plath (1932–1963)

I have done it again.
One year in every ten
I manage it——

A sort of walking miracle, my skin
Bright as a Nazi lampshade,
My right foot

A paperweight,
My face a featureless, fine
Jew linen.

Peel off the napkin
O my enemy.
Do I terrify?——

The nose, the eye pits, the full set of teeth?
The sour breath
Will vanish in a day.

Soon, soon the flesh
The grave cave ate will be
At home on me

And I a smiling woman.
I am only thirty.
And like the cat I have nine times to die.

This is Number Three.
What a trash
To annihilate each decade.

What a million filaments.
The peanut-crunching crowd
Shoves in to see

Them unwrap me hand and foot——
The big strip tease.
Gentlemen, ladies

These are my hands
My knees.
I may be skin and bone,

Nevertheless, I am the same, identical woman.
The first time it happened I was ten.
It was an accident.

The second time I meant
To last it out and not come back at all.
I rocked shut

As a seashell.
They had to call and call
And pick the worms off me like sticky pearls.

Dying
Is an art, like everything else.
I do it exceptionally well.

I do it so it feels like hell.
I do it so it feels real.
I guess you could say I've a call.

It's easy enough to do it in a cell.
It's easy enough to do it and stay put.
It's the theatrical

Comeback in broad day
To the same place, the same face, the same
        brute
Amused shout:

'A miracle!'
That knocks me out.
There is a charge

For the eyeing of my scars, there is a charge
For the hearing of my heart——
It really goes.

And there is a charge, a very large charge
For a word or a touch
Or a bit of blood

Or a piece of my hair or my clothes.
So, so, Herr Doktor.
So, Herr Enemy.

I am your opus,
I am your valuable,
The pure gold baby

That melts to a shriek.
I turn and burn.
Do not think I underestimate your great concern.

Ash, ash—
You poke and stir.
Flesh, bone, there is nothing there—

A cake of soap,
A wedding ring,
A gold filling.

Herr God, Herr Lucifer
Beware
Beware.

Out of the ash
I rise with my red hair
And I eat men like air.

23–29 OCTOBER 1962

NOW THAT I AM FOREVER WITH CHILD

audre lorde (1934–1992)

How the days went
while you were blooming within me
I remember   each upon each
the swelling changed planes of my body

how you first fluttered   then jumped
and I thought it was my heart.

How the days wound down
and the turning of winter
I recall   you
growing heavy against the wind.
I thought   now her hands
are formed   her hair
has started to curl
now her teeth are done
now she sneezes.

Then the seed opened.
I bore you one morning
just before spring
my head rang like a fiery piston
my legs were towers between which
a new world was passing.

Since then
I can only distinguish
one thread within running hours
you   flowing through selves
toward You.

MY HORSE

roque dalton (1935–1975)

I owned a horse
more beautiful and nimble than the light.

Stamping, he was like a wave of blood.
A tiny storm with eyes.
An untamed mountain on perfectly molded legs.

My horse was born dead one day
and the shock on my face put the winds to flight . . .

translated from the Spanish by Hardie St. Martin

roque dalton

When you know I'm dead don't say my name
because death and peace would stop then.

Your voice, the bell of your five senses, would form
the thin beam of light my mist would be looking for.

When you know I'm dead, say unfamiliar words.
Say flower, bee, teardrop, bread, storm.
Don't let your lips find my eleven letters.
I'm sleepy, I've loved, I've earned silence.

Don't say my name when you know I'm dead:
it would come out of the dark ground for your voice.

Don't say my name, don't say my name.
When you know I'm dead don't say my name.

translated from the Spanish by Hardie St. Martin

I COULD NOT TELL

sharon olds (b. 1942)

I could not tell I had jumped off that bus,
that bus in motion, with my child in my arms,
because I did not know it. I believed my own story:
I had fallen, or the bus had started up
when I had one foot in the air.

I would not remember the tightening of my jaw,
the rage that I'd missed my stop, the leap
into the air, the clear child
gazing about her in the air as I plunged
to one knee on the street, scraped it, twisted it,
the bus skidding to a stop, the driver
jumping out, my daughter laughing
Do it again.

        I have never done it
again. I have been very careful.
I have kept an eye on that nice young mother
who suddenly threw herself
off the moving vehicle
onto the stopped street, her life
in her hands, her life's life in her hands.

THE TALK

sharon olds

In the dark square wooden room at noon
the mother had a talk with her daughter.
The rudeness could not go on, the meanness
to her little brother, the selfishness.
The 8-year-old sat on the bed
in the corner of the room, her irises dark as
the last drops of something, her firm
face melting, reddening,
silver flashes in her eyes like distant
bodies of water glimpsed through woods.
She took it and took it and broke, crying out
I hate being a person! diving
into the mother
as if
into
a deep pond—and she cannot swim,
the child cannot swim.

ellen bryant voigt (b. 1943)

Women, women, what do they want?

The first ones in the door of the plant-filled office
were the twins, fresh from the upper grades,
their matched coats dangling open.
And then their more compliant brother, leading
the dear stuffed tottering creature—amazing
that she could lift her leg high enough
to cross the threshold to the waiting room.
Then the woman, the patient, carrying the baby
in an infant seat, his every inch of flesh
swaddled against the vicious weather.
Once inside, how skillfully the mother
unwound the many layers—

and now so quickly
must restore them: news from the lab
has passed through the nurse's sliding window.
The youngest, strapped again into his shell,
fusses for the breast, the twins tease their sister,
the eight-year-old looks almost wise as his mother
struggles into her coat with one hand and with the other
pinches his sweaty neck, her hissed threats
swarming his face like flies.

                          Now she's gone.
The women who remain don't need to speak.
Outside, snow falls in the streets
and quiet hills, and seems, in the window,
framed by the room's continuous greenery,
to obliterate the wide and varied world.
We half-smile, half-nod to one another.
One returns to her magazine.
One shifts gently to the right arm
her sleeping newborn, unfurls the bud of its hand.
One of us takes her turn in the inner office
where she submits to the steel table
and removes from her body its stubborn wish.
We want what you want, only
we have to want it more.

COULD HAVE YOU

greg moglia (b. 1943)

If my breath could catch you
Let my lungs burst with your air

If my eyes could sketch you
Let them close on your lines

If my mouth could drink you
Let your waters stream from my every pore

If my heart could have you
Let my blood laugh at its luck

linda mccarriston (b. 1943)

How graciously the animal bears pain;
she lifts her head when the small scythe
slides in her belly, looking for nothing,
closing her eyes as the slow moan
moves away from her face, then with great care
replacing her jaw on the floor.
How without notion of comfort.

greg kuzma (b. 1944)

As far away now as you ever were,
bones and a little skin.

Now rain intercedes, clouds pull back.

As far away as when you were in Georgia,
living in that broken-down house.
John there and Pat, and loud music.

Your voice lost somewhere in Colorado.

Your legs went fast uphill in California.
What was it like there?
You never said.

Rain swept along the eaves and gutters.

Into some other place you are gone.
No phone reaches you now.

The busy signal of the bees means you are gone.

Sun waking through trees, across a million miles,
means your chair is empty.

A book you read once
has flopped back closed,
the last of your breath seeps out
between its pages.

You are gone.
Your bone sticks in the ground.
Your shadow has fled from the open spaces,
to creep back under a bush.
The last of your laugh in a room
has swirled with water down the drain.
Still are you with me,
and to the ends of the earth.

THE COLONEL

carolyn forché (b. 1950)

What you have heard is true. I was in his house. His wife carried a tray of coffee and sugar. His daughter filed her nails, his son went out for the night. There were daily papers, pet dogs, a pistol on the cushion beside him. The moon swung bare on its black cord over the house. On the television was a cop show. It was in English. Broken bottles were embedded in the walls around the house to scoop the kneecaps from a man's legs or cut his hands to lace. On the windows there were gratings like those in liquor stores. We had dinner, rack of lamb, good wine, a gold bell was on the table for calling the maid. The maid brought green mangoes, salt, a type of bread. I was asked how I enjoyed the country. There was a brief commercial in Spanish. His wife took everything away. There was some talk then of how difficult it had become to govern. The parrot said hello on the terrace. The colonel told it to shut up, and pushed himself from the table. My friend said to me with his eyes: say nothing. The colonel returned with a sack used to bring groceries home. He spilled many human ears on the table. They were like dried peach halves. There is no other way to say this. He took one of them in his hands, shook it in our faces, dropped it into a water glass. It came alive there. I am tired of fooling around he said. As for the rights of anyone, tell your people they can go fuck themselves. He swept the ears to the floor with his arm and held the last of his wine in the air. Something for your poetry, no? he said. Some of the ears on the floor caught this scrap of his voice. Some of the ears on the floor were pressed to the ground.

MAY 1978

A LOVE POEM

margaret menges (b. 1951)

I wake up
in the middle of the night
and finally know exactly
where on this earth
you are
    (window   tree   door   table)

and it's enough

it is close enough

if my heart were to stop
or an artery burst open
flooding away all
the beauties I know
and if I called to you
I'm dying
        everything's leaving
           come
                please
then you would hear me

it is close enough for that

A VETERAN FATHER IN A MENTAL HOSPITAL, MINNEAPOLIS: 1995

j. e. wei (b. 1963)

for Edward Micus and his son

He is the only one you have now.
In his dream, if he walks too far to the edge of the field,
he would set a fire like his mother and run
into the corn stubs, into a pond where you couldn't fish him
    out.
If he didn't choose to live in the colorful pills' air,
he would have run like you, like the army boys,
triggering his gun at the slanting sun. You would
have heard him laugh at a clearing of the sky.
The sun creeps in—he buries his face,
like you riding a horse in that spring,
when the smoke smudged the village women's faces,
and unknown voices were white as ants crawling in a light of
    milk,
when seven yellow children were crossing the river.

And you sit on the sill, say, "Let's sleep, Willy.
Pee and let's flush the toilet."
    And Willy says, "She likes children.
    Burn a candle and bring Mom home.
    She is washing clothes by the river like their mothers.

You are a romantic poet, Dad.
You can't scold the shooting cannons.
You can't get drunk and yell down the moon.
Moon is quiet now.
Moon isn't a woman today."

A moon rests above the field.
Can you smell the air downwind?
Three deer cross the road trudging out of the shrubs.
Jeep flares blind them and the front wheels
skew and whirl one deer from the right, creaking
and cracking—the thump of the meat blurs a red flower.
To trace the light, the other two open their eyes filled with
        solid ice.
Which deer are you?

No matter how many crosses we have erected,
men cry like birches resisting the snow;
you wash the traces and wear a suit at dawn,
I will see you smile, like a fire,
like a gentle candlelight in the December sunshine.
And the wind blows: who,
who hasn't wasted his life? who,
who won't lose one or two? Children—

    killed hand in hand—
bullets whizzed by like snakes,
each fell down, mouth open for her father
or mother's name, for a second
blouses dark and faces brown,

the village was napping and no scream
rose from the valley clouds—
the burial was quiet and the bodies
flew down as if taking a breath,

silent on the plain. Silent.
You bury the water and drink the wound.
You hung the glasses and your hands dried.
Who is singing in the dark?
Inside this shut window, you hear the sun
turn away, "Willy!"
He is the only one you have now.
He has taken the moon and walks in the field.

j . e . wei

What was my mother thinking when the roosters just
   opened their eyes?
She coughed and it was her gown, the morning was cool.
She lit a fire in the kitchen, peeled onion, chopped garlic,
   stirred tofu, stripped mock duck.
She coughed and it was the sun, filtering the dust through
   our bamboo door.
Morning was a slow movie when I got up: water boiling like
   fog,
a man sweeping the road as if the night had scattered bloody
   leaves.
She crooked her back on a stool, head to the damp floor,
   seeking a leaf.

Or I had a fever—the morning table scissored a sparrow's
   shadow.
A man rang a bell in the alley; his bike squeaked.
"Selling soy beans and year cakes. Selling oil buns and Tofu
   Aah. . . ."
I opened the door, ran into the world of the sun.
I only went to the bathroom and kitchen table.
I left her in the west-side cabin, where a clock sang a tune of
   Treasure-Peace with my grandma's ancient flower. She
coughed. Her inhaler hissed.

By noon, we were chanting English in the classroom:
"Dad gets up early reading the newspaper. Mom gets up
early watering the garden rose."
Far away, a woman walked like a skunk, hands and legs
plumped, black hair and a white bag in her hand.
She opened her mouth and her wheezing I heard like a
gong.
By the window, one hundred eyes shot at her.
Whose mother is this cartoon lady, a head blooming
like a bird nest, a face with dead fish's eyes?

I bowed to the teacher, leaving the waves behind.
She knelt down and put her cheeks on mine—
her face cold like the bag. She
coughed and it was the road, extending like a log;
the sun round and the day deep like a night, where birds ate
the wings.

My classmates and the teacher laughed:
They thought she gave me a kiss.
A lunch box was warm in my hand.
They thought we were so liberal, so close and shining
like the American family in the book who had a yard like a
park,
where a boy ran like a horse.

We didn't have those mansions and American time.
We never picnicked nor went for a walk.
I only had a mother who had two bad lungs.
She coughed and it was her son.

UNTITLED

pascale giroux (b. 1967)

On the sudden I am awake,
I am in a room,
with you—Nothing I could ever contain!—
under my arm, on my chest.

You are burning with seamless entirety.

For a long second I look at your quiet face the smoothness of
the lines that draw out your open eyes.

A moment is all I can hold of you

In that moment all of you fires to the surface
every particle shows off its side, its bend.

In a moment
In the stillness,
In the warmth of your features, everything I have ever
been—
the demons,
all the faces I have worn,
all my ghosts and disguises,
all my armours and my gowns,
come out for you and yours for me.

THE NATURE OF MEMORY

kate schmitt (b. 1973)

The first thing I remember is sitting curled
against a splintering wood slat as wide as my back
inside a shed. There is sunlight like squash on the sand,
the dust in the air thrown up from your brown car.

And then looking out the back of the dirty car window
and waving my arm like a frenetic windshield wiper.

And standing in front of the huge glass, big as my room,
as planes lifted heavily into the air, each small window
cradling a face. My own face reflected in front of me,
my hands slid slowly down, making sticky tracks on the
        window.

I thought once, as it is said, that memories would flash
one by one in front of my eyes like a slideshow when I died
Each one released as the cell that contained it exploded,
then shrank to nothing.

But in your breath when you sleep,
as I watch your hood disappear flopping down the hall,
each time your face is framed in a window
I see these memories,

As if each time you leave I die.

BIOGRAPHICAL NOTES

About **Sappho** not much is known. She may have been orphaned at the age of six. She may have been a priestess or a teacher. We think she lived on the Greek island of Lesbos, in the city of Mytilene. She wrote thousands of lyrics, of which only three survive in their entirety. The rest of her work has come to us in fragments; nine volumes of her poems were lost in the sacking of Constantinople in 1204. Her lyrics were probably meant to be sung to a stringed instrument, so she is, in effect, the forerunner of today's popular female songwriters and performers. She loved women, and she wrote about her most intimate, passionate feelings regarding them. She also had a distinctive rhythmical measure in her work, now known as sapphics—a dark, eerie rhythm, consisting of thirty-eight syllables per stanza that begins something like this:

DUM da DUM DUM　DUM da da DUM
da DUM DUM　and so on.

SUGGESTED READING: *Greek Lyrics* (translated by Richmond Lattimore; University of Chicago Press). Includes poems by other ancient Greek poets as well.

Sappho: A Garland; The Poems and Fragments of Sappho (translated by Jim Powell; Farrar, Straus & Giroux).

Sappho: A New Translation (by Mary Barnard; University of California Press).

NOTE: To learn more about sapphics and other metrical stanzas and poetic forms, see Babette Deutsch's *Poetry Handbook* (Minerva Press). This is virtually an encyclopedia of poetic forms, with clear explanations and famous examples of each form.

Ch'en T'ao was the concubine of a Sung Dynasty prime minister, and from the two poems of hers that survive she seems to have had deep reservations about him. The translator, Kenneth Rexroth, has exquisitely translated many poems from both the Chinese and the Japanese.

SUGGESTED READING: *One Hundred More Poems from the Chinese: Love and the Turning Year* (translated by Kenneth Rexroth; New Directions).

Women Poets of China (translated by Kenneth Rexroth and Ling Chung; New Directions).

Rumi was a Sufi ecstatic poet who was born in what is now Afghanistan; his family fled to Turkey under threat of a Mongol invasion when Rumi was still a young man. By "ecstatic" I don't mean that Rumi was happy all the time—far from it—but at the age of thirty-seven he met a teacher, the wandering dervish Shams of Tabriz, who became his great inspiration, love, and religious guide. Later, Rumi's own followers became jealous and murdered Shams. Many of Rumi's poems are spontaneous, spoken utterances—spontaneous like the whirling dervishes, the spiritual dancers of Sufiism. He composed thousands of these poems in his lifetime.

SUGGESTED READING: *Birdsong* (fifty-three short poems translated by Coleman Barks; Maypop Press; 1-800-682-8637).

Open Secret: Versions of Rumi (translated by John Moyne and Coleman Barks; Threshold Books).

NOTE: Coleman Barks was featured on Bill Moyers' PBS poetry series *The Language of Life*. This joyful, moving, jazzy, often funny hour-long video about Rumi—"Love's Confusing Joy"—is available as part of that series. To order, call 1-800-257-5126. Many libraries carry the full series on tape, or can obtain it through interlibrary loan.

Bashō is Japan's most famous poet, and there is hardly a Japanese child who does not know this most famous frog haiku by heart. Bashō was a master of the haiku form, which many believe he perfected, and he was also a professional teacher of poetry, as well as a student of Taoism and Zen. He taught his students to go directly to the object itself: "Learn about the pines from the pine, and about bamboo from the bamboo." He instructed them to "follow nature and become a friend with things of the seasons," and to "make the universe your companion." In addition to transforming the simple verse form of the haiku (three lines of five, seven, and five syllables, respectively), he also wrote *haibun*, or travel journals, the most famous of which is probably *The Narrow Road to the Far North*.
SUGGESTED READING: *The Essential Haiku: Versions of Bashō, Buson, and Issa* (edited by Robert Hass; Ecco Press).

On Love and Barley: Haiku by Bashō (translated by Lucien Stryk; Penguin).

NOTE: For further information about the haiku form, try, in addition to the Hass book, *The Haiku Handbook* (by William J. Higginson with Penny Harter; Kodansha).

After the English poet **William Blake**'s death, his wife, Katherine, continued to speak to him as if he were standing out in the backyard with her. Blake himself had conversations with invisible beings most of his life—as a child, he was punished for telling his mother that he saw angels in the trees outside their house. During his lifetime, his work both as poet and print-maker was ignored and even ridiculed. He called himself an "enthusiastic, hope-fostered visionary" and proclaimed: "I know that This World is a World of imagination & Vision. I see Every thing I paint in This World, but Every body does not see alike."

SUGGESTED READING: *Blake: Complete Writings* (edited by Geoffrey Keynes; Oxford University Press). Includes poems, essays, annotations, and letters.

Songs of Innocence and of Experience (with an introduction and commentary by Geoffrey Keynes; Orion Press). A reproduction, with color plates, of William Blake's "illuminated" book.

Issa's mother died when he was only two years old, and when Issa was fourteen his father hired him out as an apprentice in Edo (the former name of Tokyo). Issa spent much of his life wandering through the country. In addition to writing haiku, Issa wrote a few heartbreakingly beautiful travel journals, *haibun*, of which the best, *The Year of My Life*, alas, is now out of print. Excerpts from this diary appear in Robert Hass's *The Essential Haiku*, along with many of Issa's best haiku poems. Issa's life was in many ways tragic—four of his children died before the age of three—and yet he wrote with tenderness and compassion about insects, birds, and human beings. He often chastised himself for being a bad Buddhist, wasting "days and months in meaningless activity." Beyond that, he wrote: "Try as I would, I could not, simply could not, cut the binding cord of human love."

SUGGESTED READING: *The Essential Haiku: Versions of Bashō, Buson, and Issa* (edited by Robert Hass; Ecco Press).

The Year of My Life: A Translation of Issa's Oraga Haru (translated by Noboyuki Yuasa; University of California Press; out of print).

Friedrich Hölderlin knew many of the most famous German philosophers and poets of his time, including Goethe, Schiller, and Hegel. In 1796 he became a tutor for a wealthy Frankfurt banker named Gontard, and fell hopelessly in love with the banker's young wife, Susette, whom he nicknamed "Diotima" (after the teacher who Socrates claimed revealed to him the true nature of love). She died of pneumonia in 1802, the same year that Hölderlin returned from a long walking trip through Europe looking "pale as a corpse, emaciated, with hollow wide eyes, long hair and a beard, and dressed like a beggar." He never fully recovered his sanity, and spent the last thirty-five years of his life living alone in a tower in Tübingen, Germany, under the care of a local carpenter. He published poems and a verse play, wrote at least part of a novel, and translated the ancient Greek poets into German. About poetry, Hölderlin once wrote in a letter to his brother that "it unites people if it is authentic and works authentically, with all the manifold suffering, fortune, striving, hoping and fearing, with all their opinions and mistakes, all their virtues and ideas, with everything major and minor that exists among them, unites them into a living, a thousand times divided, inward whole." This, he said, "shall be poetry itself."

SUGGESTED READING: *Hymns and Fragments* (translated and introduced by Richard Sieburth; Princeton University Press).

Friedrich Hölderlin: Essays and Letters on Theory (translated and edited by Thomas Pfau; SUNY Press).

This **Hebrew folk song** is found in a wide variety of Jewish songbooks. Rabbi Nachman of Bratzlav, to whom these words are attributed, was a man famous for his fervency and for his moral parables. He was born in Mizhbozh, Podolia (Russia). He is still much beloved by the Hassidic sect known as the Bratzlavs, who consider him their living Rebbe. Hasidism itself is a branch of Torah observant Judaism that developed in the eighteenth century in the Ukraine and Poland. Its founder was known as the Baal Shem Tov, and the movement centered around rediscovering heartfelt worship, simplicity, and mystical joy in religion. The translation of this song is literal, and in its very clunkiness lies its poetry. The melody to this song is simple and beautiful, and the two lines are sung over and over.

SUGGESTED READING: *Tales of the Hasidim* (by Martin Buber; Schocken Books).

Yiddish Wisdom: Yiddishe Cochma (illustrated by Kristina Swarner; Chronicle Books).

Nine and a Half Mystics (by Herbert Weiner; Collier Books).

The English poet **John Keats** was dead by the age of twenty-five, of tuberculosis, then known as "consumption." He left behind a few long poems and several exquisite odes, as well as shorter lyrics like the ones included here. "This Living Hand" is the last poem he composed, which he wrote to Fanny Brawne, the woman whom he loved and was secretly engaged to, but he didn't live long enough to marry. In a letter to his brother George he once wrote that life itself and all its trouble is "Soul making," an education of the soul. "Do you not see how necessary a World of pains and troubles is to school an Intelligence and make it a Soul?" His books were scorned by contemporary critics, and he thought himself a miserable failure. He composed his own epitaph accordingly: "Here lies one whose name was writ in water."
SUGGESTED READING: *The Essential Keats* (selected by Philip Levine; Ecco Press).

John Keats: Selected Poetry and Letters (with an introduction by Richard Harter Fogle; Rinehart & Company; out of print).

Alfred, Lord Tennyson was made Poet Laureate of England in 1850. Long before that, however, when he was still a young man, his best friend, Arthur Hallam, drowned at sea. Tennyson wrote a number of poems over the course of several years, trying to come to terms with that loss, and those poems collectively are called *In Memoriam*. He wrote many other poems as well, long narrative poems and short lyrics. As a small boy, he liked to make himself

ant the mind of others," and also "my ears are only comfortable
hen the singer sings as if mere speech had taken fire."
GGESTED READING: *Early Poems Unabridged* (Dover Thrift Edi-
n).

lected Poems and Two Plays of William Butler Yeats* (edited and
th an introduction by M. L. Rosenthal; Collier Books).

OTE: You can hear Yeats reading his own poetry and speaking "as
mere speech had taken fire," along with others discussing and
ading his work, on the audiotape *The Poems of William Butler
ats* (Spoken Arts; available from the Poets' Audio Center, P.O.
x 50145, Washington, DC 20004).

e poet **Rainer Marie Rilke** was born in Prague. At the age of
enty-one he went about "wearing an old-world frock coat, black
avat, and broad-brimmed black hat, clasping a long-stemmed iris
d smiling, oblivious of the passersby, a forlorn smile into ineffa-
e horizons." He worked for a time as secretary to the French
ulptor Auguste Rodin. As a poet, he would sometimes go for
ars without writing and then, as in the winter of 1922, write in
rush of poetry, including the fifty-nine *Sonnets to Orpheus*
d the last of the *Duino Elegies*. In his famous *Letters to a Young
et* he told his young friend: "No one can advise or help you—no
e. There is only one thing you should do. Go into yourself. Find
t the reason that commands you to write; see whether it has
read its roots into the very depths of your soul; admit to yourself if
u would die should you be forbidden to write. This most of all:
k yourself in the deep silence of night: *must* I write . . . if you an-
er "*I must,*" then build your life in accordance with that neces-
ty. . . ."
GGESTED READING: *Letters to a Young Poet* (translated by
ephen Mitchell; Vintage).

dizzy by repeating his own name over and over and spinning himself around in a circle till he forgot himself. (Compare with the
Sufi poet Rumi, above.)
SUGGESTED READING: *In Memoriam* (Norton Critical Edition, with
annotations and criticism; Norton).

NOTE: The folk singer Loreena McKenna has set some of Tennyson's lyrics to haunting music. My favorite is her "Lady of
Shalott," on a tape called *The Visit* (Warner Brothers). This is the
one students most often ask to borrow.

Walt Whitman, an American poet, worked most of his adult life on
a single book of poems, *Leaves of Grass*, which he kept revising and
published in six different editions. He worked a number of jobs—
teacher, printer, newspaperman—and he voluntarily nursed in-
jured soldiers during the Civil War, reading to them, writing letters
home, and bringing little gifts of coins, stamps, and ice cream
(which, on one hot day, he carried from ward to ward). In his preface to *Leaves of Grass* he wrote that a poet "judges not as the
judge . . . but as sunlight falling around a helpless thing." He gave
advice in that preface, too: "This is what you shall do: Love the
earth and sun and the animals, despise riches, give alms to every
one that asks, stand up for the stupid and crazy, devote your
income and labor to others, hate tyrants . . . re-examine all you
have been told at school or church or in any book, dismiss whatever
insults your own soul, and your very flesh shall be a great
poem. . . ."
SUGGESTED READING: *The Essential Whitman* (selected by Galway
Kinnell; Ecco Press).

The Portable Walt Whitman (revised and enlarged edition; edited
by Mark Van Doren; Penguin). Contains the complete *Leaves of
Grass*, as well as essays, sketches, prefaces, and other writings.

The Gift (by Lewis Hyde; Vintage). See especially chapter nine: "A Draft of Whitman," the most succinct and lyrical reading of Whitman's poetry and life I know.

Walt Whitman: The Making of the Poet (by Paul Zweig; Basic Books). This wonderful biography and reading of the work is, alas, out of print, but may be found in most libraries. If it's not at your local branch, try asking for it through interlibrary loan.

Charles Baudelaire was a French poet who managed to shock almost everyone, though he ended his short, often unhappy life as a docile Catholic convert and an invalid, driven around Paris in his mother's carriage. He introduced the French to the work of the American author and poet Edgar Allan Poe, and published one book of his own verse, *Les Fleurs du mal*, and a book of prose poems translated as *Paris Spleen*. His work influenced a number of literary movements, including the Symbolists, the Surrealists, and the Dadaists. Of the prose poem form he wrote to a friend: "Which one of us, in moments of ambition, has not dreamed of the miracle of a poetic prose, musical, without rhythm and without rhyme, supple and rugged enough to adapt itself to the lyrical impulses of the soul, the undulations of dreams, the prickings of consciousness?"
SUGGESTED READING: *Flowers of Evil and Other Works / Les Fleurs du Mal et Oeuvres Choisies: A Dual Language Book* (Dover Books).

Paris Spleen (translated by Louise Varese; New Directions).

Matthew Arnold was famous both as a poet and a critic in his day. He was the son of an English clergyman and became first an inspector of elementary schools and then a professor of poetry at Oxford, where he stopped writing great poetry, turning instead to essays, criticism, and bad verse. He wrote that poetry, "to be capable of fulfilling such high destinies, must be poetry of a high order

of excellence," and that the "best poetry" may l
its "truth and seriousness."
SUGGESTED READING: *Poetry and Criticism o*
(edited by A. Dwight Culler; Riverside Bookshe

Emily Dickinson was an American poet who le:
Amherst, Massachusetts, only once—and briefly
in nearby Holyoke. In later years, she seldom le:
times not even her room, and she dressed all in
wrote hundreds of poems, on tiny scraps of pape
writing, she published less than a handful of th(
When a friend once asked if she sometimes long
she told him, "I never thought of conceiving tha
the slightest approach to such a want in all fu|
pause she added, "I feel that I have not express
enough." "I find ecstasy in living," she told him.
of living is joy enough." It was not till after her d
was published in book form—by the same pe
jected it during her life—and not till 1955 that l
lished as she actually wrote it, with its pec
half-rhymes. The work here is from that definitiv
SUGGESTED READING: *The Complete Poems of*
(edited by Thomas H. Johnson; Little, Brown).
tive variorum edition of 1955.

Selected Poems and Letters of Emily Dickinson
Co.).

In addition to poems, **William Butler Yeats** wrot
(his father was a famous painter), and recorded Ir
folklore. He helped to found the famous Abbey T
and was a leader in the Irish Renaissance move
tensely interested in magic and the occult, and (
that "the poet binds with a spell his own mind wl

Selected Poems of Rainer Maria Rilke (translation and commentary by Robert Bly; HarperCollins).

The source for the **three Spanish folk songs** is unclear, though it is believed that the anonymous folk authors here may be women. There are thousands of such song-poems in Spanish. These were first collected by the Spanish scholar Francisco Rodríguez Marín in 1882 and published in Madrid, Spain, under the title *Cantos populares de Español*. The translator here, Martin Bidney, a scholar and professor of English literature at the State University of New York at Binghamton, first encountered these poems in Russian. He has also translated other poems from the Russian, and has written articles about poets William Blake, Walt Whitman, and many others.

SUGGESTED READING: If you know Spanish, get hold of *Cantos populares de Español*, and do your own translations! Martin Bidney and his teenage daughter, Sarah, have been translating these poems together for years.

The American-born poet **Ezra Pound** was born in Idaho and raised in Pennsylvania, and then moved to Europe, where, according to one of his contemporaries, he used to wear "trousers made of green billiard cloth, a pink coat, a blue shirt, a tie handpainted by a Japanese friend, an immense sombrero, a flaming beard cut to a point [he had bright red hair] and a single, large blue earring." He befriended many then unknown poets (among them T. S. Eliot and Robert Frost) and founded a number of literary movements, including Vorticism and Imagism. Regarding Imagism, wrote Pound, "The artist seeks out the luminous detail and presents it. He does not comment." "In a Station of the Metro" was originally thirty lines long, and Pound revised it to two lines. Said Pound, "In a poem of this sort one is trying to record the precise instant when a thing outward and objective transforms itself, or darts into a thing inward and subjective."

During World War II Pound went on the radio broadcasting propaganda on behalf of Fascist Italy, and after the war was brought back to the United States, where he was charged with treason and spent thirteen years locked up in St. Elizabeth's for the insane. Because of his virulent anti-Semitism and his pro-Fascist activities during the war he remains a highly controversial figure in American letters. In his later years he told the visiting poet Allen Ginsberg, "The worst mistake I ever made was that stupid, suburban prejudice of anti-Semitism."

SUGGESTED READING: *Literary Essays of Ezra Pound* (edited with an introduction by T. S. Eliot; New Directions).

Selected Poems of Ezra Pound (New Directions).

The Russian poet **Anna Akhmatova** lived through the Stalinist terrors of the 1930s—where students, artists, intellectuals, and dissidents of all kinds were imprisoned or killed. Her work was banned in the Soviet Union for much of her life, officially and unofficially; her son was imprisoned; her first husband was executed for anti-Bolshevik activities; and many of her closest friends—fellow poets—were victims of the same repression. For years, her poem "Requiem" existed only in her own memory and that of a few close friends. She was famous for her bravery, strength, and elegance. Here is a description of her by a lifelong friend: "an elegant young woman with . . . large, deep, brightly sparkling eyes standing out strangely against the background of her black hair and dark brows and lashes. She was a sparkling water sprite, an avid wanderer on foot, climbed like a cat, and swam like a fish."

SUGGESTED READING: *Anna Ahkmatova: Selected Poems* (translated by D. M. Thomas; Penguin). D. M. Thomas is a noted poet and novelist, author of *The White Hotel* and other works.

Twenty Poems of Anna Akhmatova (translated by Jane Kenyon; Ally/The Eighties Press). Jane Kenyon, herself an earth-shattering poet, translated only twenty of Akhmatova's poems, but did so exquisitely. Ms. Kenyon died in 1995 of leukemia. Her entire book of new and selected poems, *Otherwise* (Graywolf Press), is itself vital reading for any lover of poetry.

César Vallejo, a Peruvian poet, lived an almost impossibly difficult life. He left the poor mining town in northern Peru where he was raised to go to college and when he returned home became involved, against his will, in a local political feud. The result for him was a three-month jail sentence. After his second book of poems was published he lost his teaching job in Lima, and went off to Paris to spend the rest of his life in dismal poverty. He made an art of learning how not to wear out the soles of one's shoes, to live as cheaply as possible. He became a committed Marxist, and died, exactly as he had predicted, on a rainy day in Paris.
SUGGESTED READING: *Neruda and Vallejo: Selected Poems* (edited and with a new preface by Robert Bly; HarperCollins).

Federico García Lorca was born into a wealthy family in Granada, Spain. He went to school on winter mornings in an elegant red cape with a black fur collar, but early on became acutely aware of the poverty and suffering of others, and it turned him against both the politicians and the Catholic Church of his day. Lorca loved Spanish folk music, gypsy dances, and the rich, dreamlike imagery of Surrealism, a school of art he helped to found in Madrid, where he met H. G. Wells, Albert Einstein, Marie Curie, Picasso, and Salvador Dalí, among others. He was a pianist, artist, actor, director, political activist, and writer of plays, prose poems, newspaper articles, lectures, opera libretti, and, of course, poems. "Intelligence is often the enemy of poetry," he wrote, "because it limits too much, and it elevates the poet to a sharp-edged throne where he forgets that ants could eat him or that a great arsenic lobster could fall on his head." In 1936, during the last days of the Spanish Civil War, the thirty-eight-year-old poet was hunted down by right-wing Fascist forces and, under orders of one of Franco's generals, was executed by a firing squad.

SUGGESTED READING: *Federico García Lorca: Collected Poems* (a bilingual edition; edited by Christopher Maurer; Farrar, Straus & Giroux).

Langston Hughes was born in Joplin, Missouri. He was a vital figure in the Black Harlem Renaissance Movement, a spokesperson for civil rights, a dynamic lecturer, and a writer of poems, stories, autobiography, jazz lyrics, essays, plays, humor, and children's literature. After graduating from high school, he spent a year in Mexico, then studied at Columbia University for a time, though he completed his B.A. at Lincoln University in Pennsylvania. He was named "class poet" in his elementary school, and published his first poem in a national magazine at the age of nineteen. In public readings, he often performed his poetry to jazz accompaniment.

Few poets have been as beloved by their native country-folk as the Chilean poet **Pablo Neruda**. In a memoir, Neruda tells this story from his childhood: "I came upon a hole in one of the boards of the fence. . . . All of a sudden a hand appeared— a tiny hand of a boy about my own age. By the time I came close again, the hand was gone, and in its place was a marvellous white wool sheep." He explains that he "went into the house and brought out a treasure of my own: a pinecone, opened, full of odor and resin, which I adored. . . . That exchange brought home to me for the first time a precious idea: that all of humanity is somehow together. . . . Maybe this smell and mysterious exchange of gifts remained inside me also, deep and indestructible, giving my poetry light."

Neruda worked tirelessly, sometimes furiously, for social justice and democracy. He was elected to the Chilean Senate from the mining territory of Chile, his term of office ending (in

1948) when he was declared a "traitor" and began to be hounded by right-wing Secret Police. It was miners and other workers who saved his life by passing him secretly from house to house. In 1971 he received the Nobel Prize for literature, but in 1973 there was a military coup against his close friend, Chilean president Salvador Allende. The military despised Neruda but didn't know what to do about him, as he was then in a hospital, being treated for cancer. Not daring to harm him directly, they ordered all medical treatment stopped. Within a few days Neruda died, and his home and study were vandalized by military thugs. That house remains a shrine for many Chileans and others who come to visit the place where Neruda lived and worked: "in Isla Negra, the sea, / all of its thunder, its floating hardware, / its tons of salt."

SUGGESTED READING: *The Captain's Verses* (translated by Donald D. Walsh; New Directions). Many of Neruda's best love poems are included in this volume.

Neruda and Vallejo: Selected Poems (edited and with a new preface by Robert Bly; HarperCollins).

NOTE: The recent Italian movie *Il Postino (The Postman)* features a fictionalized account of the friendship between Pablo Neruda and a local village mail carrier. This summary doesn't begin to suggest the charm of the movie, which also features some of Neruda's most beautiful poems. Happily, there is also an audiotape of *Il Postino* (Miramax) that features music and poems from the film along with other Neruda poems read by such performers as Julia Roberts, Sting, Andy Garcia, and Madonna (who reads "If You Forget Me" beautifully).

Czeslaw Milosz was born in Lithuania. He began to write and publish his work as an undergraduate, earned his law degree, and was active in the anti-Nazi underground in Poland during World

War II. Later he acted as a diplomat for the Communists, but defected from Poland in 1951, first to Paris and then to the United States. All this had led him to remark that "history is extremely real." Author of poems, criticism, novels, translations, and essays, he is a member of the American Academy of the Institute of Arts and Letters and won the Nobel Prize for literature in 1980. Of his work he has said, "It turns out that all my work has gone against the grain. In a certain sense, I was sticking out my tongue at the world . . . but I wasn't thumbing my nose, not jeering."

Muriel Rukeyser, poet, activist, and feminist, was born in New York City. At the age of nineteen she was arrested in Alabama for protesting at the famous trial of the "Scottsboro Boys," nine black youths falsely accused of raping two white women. Three years later, she traveled to the deadly silica mines of West Virginia, recording in prose and poetry the betrayal of the miners by corporate interests. She spoke out during the Spanish Civil War (see the note on poet Federico García Lorca, above), and worked tirelessly on behalf of a South Korean poet condemned to death for political protest. She was also a biographer, playwright, children's book writer, president of PEN (an international writer's organization that works on behalf of human rights), and mother of one son. About the need for poetry in our lives she wrote: "I wish to say that we will not be saved by poetry. But poetry is the type of creation in which we may live and which will save us."
SUGGESTED READING: *The Life of Poetry* (Paris Press). Beautiful essays about life and poetry and the vital connections between them.

Out of Silence (Triquarterly Books).

Robert Lowell, an American poet, was a member of the famous Lowell family of Boston (James Russell Lowell, Amy Lowell, and others). He won the Pulitzer Prize for literature in 1946 for his book of poems *Lord Weary's Castle* but is probably most famous as one of the leaders of the Confessional school of poetry—devoted to intense, passionate, agonizing poems of autobiography. He was the teacher of poets Sylvia Plath, Anne Sexton, Maxine Kumin, and others.

SUGGESTED READING: *Selected Poems* (Farrar, Straus & Giroux).

Jack Gilbert was born in Pittsburgh, Pennsylvania, and was the 1962 winner of the Yale Younger Poet Series for his first book, *Views of Jeopardy*. This and his second book, *Monolithos*, were both nominated for the Pulitzer Prize in poetry. His newest book, in which the poem "Married" appears, *The Great Fires: Poems 1982–1992*, contains many poems about the death of his wife, Michiko Nogami, and is dedicated to her.

SUGGESTED READING: *The Great Fires: Poems 1982–1992* (Knopf).

Galway Kinnell spent his childhood in Pawtucket, Rhode Island. He attended Princeton University and the University of Rochester. He served in the U.S. Navy, was arrested in Louisiana in 1963 working for civil rights, and in the late 1960s was an active protestor against the war in Vietnam. He is currently professor of English and creative writing at New York University. He has translated poems by the French poet François Villon and published a novel, *Black Light*, as well as essays, interviews, and twelve books of poems. Mr. Kinnell encourages his students to handwrite and memorize poems—to learn them "by hand, by heart and by mouth." He has commented: "The death of the self I seek, in poetry and out of poetry, is . . . a death out of which one might hope to be reborn more giving, more alive, more open, more related to the natural life."

SUGGESTED READING: *The Book of Nightmares* (Houghton Mifflin).

Selected Poems (Houghton Mifflin).

Walking Down the Stairs: Selections from Interviews (University of Michigan Press).

NOTE: Galway Kinnell is a superb reader (and reciter) of his own work. There are several audio- and videotapes of Mr. Kinnell reading from his work, including the audio recording titled *The Poetry and Voice of Galway Kinnell* (Caedmon).

James Wright was born in Martin's Ferry, Ohio. He graduated from Kenyon College, and earned a doctorate from the University of Washington, in Seattle. In addition to writing his own poems, he also translated poems from the German, Spanish, and Chinese. He won the Pulitzer Prize for his *Collected Poems* in 1972. Beginning in the 1960s, Wright began to work in what some people call "the deep image"—startling leaps of imagination and beauty.
SUGGESTED READING: *Collected Poems* (New England Press).

This Journey (Vintage). This was James Wright's last book of poems, which he finished just before his death; it was, in fact, put together posthumously with the help of his wife, Annie, and poets Galway Kinnell, Donald Hall, Jane Kenyon, and others.

Philip Levine, one of twin brothers, was born in Detroit, Michigan, and spent a working-class childhood and youth in that industrial city. He taught for more than thirty years at California State University in Fresno. His book of poems *What Work Is* won the National Book Award in 1991. He edited *The Essential Keats* (see John Keats) and his latest book of poems, *The Simple Truth*, won a Pulitzer Prize in 1995.
SUGGESTED READING: *The Simple Truth* (Knopf).

What Work Is (Knopf).

The Bread of Time (Knopf). Memoirs and personal essays.

NOTE: The Lannan Foundation has produced a videotape of Philip Levine reading from and discussing his work. For information on this, as well as dozens of other tapes of contemporary poets including Carolyn Forché and Sharon Olds, write to the Lannan Foundation, 5401 McConnell Avenue, Los Angeles, CA 90066-7027.

Sylvia Plath, an American poet, committed suicide on February 11, 1963. She was at that time separated from her husband, the poet Ted Hughes, and was struggling to manage alone with two small children in a cold flat in London. Her father had killed himself when she was a child. She attended Smith College, and acted as a young guest editor for *Mademoiselle* magazine, an experience she partly recalls in her famous novel *The Bell Jar*.
SUGGESTED READING: *The Bell Jar* (HarperCollins).

The Collected Poems (HarperCollins).

African-American poet **Audre Lorde** was born in New York City and lived there much of her life. She was a militant and impassioned spokesperson for her race, her gender, and lesbian love. "Our poems formulate the implications of ourselves, what we feel within and dare to make real . . . our fears, our hopes, our most cherished terrors." She died in 1992.
SUGGESTED READING: *Audre Lorde: Chosen Poems, Old and New* (Norton).

The Cancer Journals (Spinsters, Ink). In this book, Ms. Lorde recorded her struggles with the breast cancer that eventually killed her.

Roque Dalton, the El Salvadoran poet and revolutionary, was born in San Salvador. Even as a student he protested the injustices of the military dictatorships in his country. He was arrested several times, and exiled to Mexico. Twice he escaped execution for his revolutionary activities. Ironically, he was killed in 1975 by a military faction of his own left-wing revolutionary group, and thrown into a shallow grave in a dump where many victims of the right-wing death squads had been disposed of. He once said in an interview that he had "an urgent need to say many things about my country, about man." He also said that "what I expect to go on being until I die is a revolutionary poet truly conscious of the problems of his time." He was killed four days before his fortieth birthday.

SUGGESTED READING: *Small Hours of the Night: Selected Poems* (edited by Hardie St. Martin; Curbstone Press). The poem "Small Hours of the Night" appears in a slightly different version in the book.

Poet **Sharon Olds** was born in San Francisco. She has published five collections of poems. She teaches at New York University's Graduate Program in Creative Writing and for the past thirteen years has helped to run a workshop for the severely physically disabled at Goldwater Memorial Hospital on Roosevelt Island.

SUGGESTED READING: *Satan Says* (University of Pittsburgh Press).

The Wellspring (Knopf).

Ellen Bryant Voigt, an American poet, founded and directed the original low-residency M.F.A. writing program at Goddard College and now teaches at its new incarnation at Warren Wilson College in North Carolina. She has published five books of poems and has written, "The image, then, can reproduce not only what the poet sees but at the same time *how* the poet sees. . . ."

SUGGESTED READING: *The Forces of Plenty* (Norton).

The Lotus Flowers (Norton).

The Wide and Varied World (Norton).

Greg Moglia grew up in New York City, the child of Italian-American parents. "There is so much we know, but do not know we know. Poetry taps into a special part of each of us. It surprises, then comforts, by telling us how much knowledge is at our fingertips." He teaches education courses at New York University, and also physics, psychology, and philosophy at East Rockaway High School, on Long Island, New York.

Linda McCarriston was featured on Bill Moyers's PBS poetry series, *The Language of Life*. She grew up in a working-class family in Lynn, Massachusetts, and has written about women, children, animals, healing, and the domestic violence she witnessed and experienced growing up. About her poetry she has said, "I tried again and again to write these poems, and I was really driven a little bit wild by the *necessity* to write them." She has also observed, "Poetry allows one to speak with a voice of power that is not, in fact, granted to one by the culture."
SUGGESTED READING: *Eva-Mary* (TriQuarterly Books).

Talking Soft Dutch (Texas Tech University Press).

NOTE: It is worth looking for both the videotape, in which Ms. McCarriston reads and discusses her poems, and the book *The Language of Life* (Doubleday), in which her work and words appear.

Greg Kuzma is the author of more than twenty books of poems. He lives in Crete, Nebraska, and has for many years taught poetry-writing at the University of Nebraska in Lincoln. He recently finished a play about the poet Delmore Schwartz, and another about the composer and performer Franz Liszt. He is currently putting together a volume of selected poems and a collection of his longer poems.
SUGGESTED READING: *Grandma—a poem* (Best Cellar Press).

Of China and of Greece (Sun; 347 West 39th Street, NYC, NY 10018).

Carolyn Forché, poet, translator, editor, and activist, worked for a time in the 1970s as an aide-de-camp in El Salvador. (See the experiences of poet Roque Dalton, above). There she saw the atrocities inflicted by right-wing death squads, and returned to this country to "bear witness" here and abroad. She has visited Lebanon and Ireland to report on activities there, and has lived in France, Latin America, and California. She now lives with her husband and son near Washington, D.C., and teaches in the creative writing program at George Mason University in Virginia. Her first book of poems, *Gathering the Tribes*, won the Yale Younger Series Award, and her second, *The Country Between Us*, a book largely about her experiences in El Salvador, won the Lamont Poetry Award. Of her most recent work she has written: "The first-person, free-verse, lyric-narrative poem of my earlier years has given way to a work which has desired its own bodying forth: polyphonic, broken, haunted, and in ruins, with no possibility of restoration."
SUGGESTED READING: *The Angel of History* (Norton).

The Country Between Us (HarperCollins).

NOTE: Carolyn Forché is editor of *Against Forgetting: Twentieth-Century Poetry of Witness* (Norton; pbk.). This is one of the most powerful books of twentieth-century poetry available, representing not only British and American poets but poets of many other languages and countries.

Margaret Menges lives in Elmira, New York, where she teaches middle school and lives with her two teenaged sons. This is her first published poem. She writes, "The world is so exquisite and it sings a thousand melodies to us in the course of a day. To me, poetry is stepping back from the world in order to be more intensely a part of it. Through poetry, I get to sing back. . . ."

J. E. Wei grew up in a village in southern Taiwan that he calls a "Plum-Flower-Paradise, filled with mountains, rivers, trees, birds, and children's laughter and dreams." His father was a doctor in the village, and Wei himself was a medical student for a brief time. He earned a master's degree in literature and creative writing at the University of Minnesota and is currently studying poetry-writing in the Ph.D. program at the State University of New York at Binghamton. Of poetry, he says it is "a lifetime companion, with whom I travel in time—we wake up together and go for a walk. Poetry knows me and guides me so well that when I sleep, this loyal friend talks to all of the people and objects I have cared for and treasured somewhere in the dark."

Pascale Giroux grew up in Paris, one of five sisters. The family moved to New York City when Pascale was twelve. She currently lives in San Francisco, where she teaches middle school. "Poetry has always been a private language for me. The one that breathes inside my body and continuously, quietly speaks the truth."

Kate Schmitt was raised in New England but spent part of her childhood in Singapore and Hong Kong. "From the time I was a child I buried myself in books. I read for those moments that nearly broke me apart because they were so perfect. They captured something that I didn't realize other people even felt. They made my own mind make more sense to me. Writing poetry for me is like opening up onto paper and gathering all the things inside and around me and trying to figure it all out." She earned her bachelor's degree from Colgate University and worked in publishing for a time in Boston before she moved to Hong Kong to live with her sister, then to teach for a year in mainland China. She is attending graduate school in Houston, Texas. This is her first published poem.

OTHER BOOKS THAT
MAY BE OF INTEREST

The Practice of Poetry: Writing Exercises from Poets Who Teach (edited by Robin Behn and Chase Twitchell; HarperCollins). A handbook of writing exercises, this book is full of ideas, suggestions, examples, and games from poets who spend their lives helping other poets to loosen up, get started, and stretch their abilities.

The Voice That Is Great Within Us: American Poetry of the Twentieth Century (edited by Hayden Carruth; Bantam). A generous and thorough sampling of twentieth-century American poetry, arranged chronologically, with helpful notes by the award-winning poet Hayden Carruth.

Poetry Handbook: A Dictionary of Terms (by Babette Deutsch; Minerva Press; fourth edition). A virtual encyclopedia of poetic terms and forms—ballades, double dactyls, sonnets, villanelles, you name it—complete with clear explanations and some of the world's greatest examples of each form.

A Celebration of Bees (by Barbara Juster Esbensen; Henry Holt). An exuberant introduction to poetry, complete with examples, ideas, and exercises, for young poets of every age. Includes many examples from the young poets themselves.

These Small Stones (poems selected by Norma Farber and Myra Cohn Livingston; HarperCollins). This is a superb collection of short and very short poems for young readers by two of America's most dedicated children's poetry anthologists.

Field Days (edited by Lee Bennett Hopkins; Harcourt Brace). Wherever I go, young people are always asking for poems about sports. This is a whole book full of them, by America's most indefatigable anthologizer of children's poetry. Mr. Hopkins has also edited a beautiful selection of Carl Sandburg's poems for young readers, among many, many other collections.

The Norton Introduction to Poetry (edited by J. Paul Hunter; Norton; fifth edition). Mr. Hunter, a noted scholar, editor, and teacher, has been using this constantly updated book in his own college classes for years. It is a thorough, intelligent, and generous introduction to poetry in the English language.

The Place My Words Are Looking For (selected by Paul Janeczko; Bradbury Press). Mr. Janeczko may well be the teenage poet's best friend—he has done more and better anthologies for the young adult reader than any poet alive. This one includes poems, photos, and commentaries by a wide variety of American poets, a mix of those who write mostly for children (Jack Prelutsky, Lillian Morrison) and those who write mostly for adults (Jim Daniels, William Stafford).

Rose, Where Did You Get That Red?: Teaching Great Poetry to Children (by Kenneth Koch; Vintage). This is the classic book on teaching poems to young people, and on finding ways for those poems to become springboards for writing poetry. It is a gentle introduction to great poems, complete with examples of work from the young poets whom Mr. Koch taught over many years. Mr. Koch, with Kate Farrell, has also gathered a wonderful anthology of verse for young readers called *Sleeping on the Wing* (Vintage/Random House).

Smart Like Me: High School–Age Writing from the Sixties to Now (edited by Dick Lourie and Mark Pawlak, with Robert Hershon and Ron Schreiber; Hanging Loose Press). For more than thirty years, the journal *Hanging Loose* has provided a forum for high school–age writers to appear side by side with some of our best contemporary authors. *Smart Like Me* is a selection of the young writers' poems from that publication, dating from the 1960s to the present. *Hanging Loose,* now up to its seventieth issue, is a triquarterly publication that every high school–age writer should know. The address is: Hanging Loose Press, 231 Wyckoff Street, Brooklyn, NY 11217. If you want to send work, read the magazine first, and remember to send a self-addressed stamped envelope!

Lifelines (edited by Leonard Marcus; Orchard Books). A moving collection of poems for young readers, organized thematically.

The Invisible Ladder: An Anthology of Contemporary American Poems for Young Readers (edited by Liz Rosenberg; Henry Holt). A beautiful selection of the best contemporary American poets (Alice Walker, Robert Bly, Allen Ginsberg, and others). Complete with fine comments by the contributors, as well as childhood *and* contemporary photographs of the poets. I would love this book even if I hadn't edited it.

Contemporary American Poets (edited by Mark Strand; New American Library). A gem of a collection of American poetry since 1940, arranged alphabetically by author, and selected by one of America's finest poets.

Writing Poems (edited by Robert Wallace and Michelle Boisseau; HarperCollins; fourth edition). For the more sophisticated reader, a college-level introduction to poetry—the poems themselves, as well as terms and techniques, ranging from voice to meter to persona to metaphor and simile. Wonderful explanations, examples, and exercises.

INDEX OF AUTHORS

INDEX OF FIRST LINES

The bull does not know you, nor the fig tree, 42

The first ones in the door of the plant-filled office, 74

The first thing I remember is sitting curled, 89

There are blows in life so violent—I can't answer, 34

There I learned how faces fall apart, 30

The sea is calm to-night, 21

The way of love is not / a subtle argument, 6

The whole world is a very narrow bridge, 13

The wind is cruel. Her clothes are worn and thin, 4

This living hand, now warm and capable, 15

This world of dew, 11

We have no idea what his fantastic head, 27

We were riding through frozen fields in a wagon at dawn, 47

What happens to a dream deferred, 44

What have you eaten / that's made you so pale, 28

What was my mother thinking when the roosters just opened their eyes, 86

What you have heard is true. I was in his house, 80

When I wrote of the women in their dances and wildness, it was a mask, 48

When they brought me the news / that you don't love me, 28

When you are old and gray and full of sleep, 26

When you know I'm dead don't say my name, 71

Wild Nights—Wild Nights! / Were I with thee, 23

Word over all, beautiful as the sky, 18

You cry, waking from a nightmare, 55

Liz Rosenberg has published two books of poems, *The Fire Music* and *Children of Paradise* (University of Pittsburgh Press), as well as more than a dozen children's picture books, one previous poetry anthology for young readers called *The Invisible Ladder* (Holt), and a young adult novel titled *Heart and Soul* (Harcourt Brace). Her work has won many awards, including the Agnes Starrett Poetry Prize, the Patterson Prize, an IRA Children's Choice Award, and a grant from the Pennsylvania Council of the Arts. She teaches the creative writing program at the State University of New York at Binghamton and has traveled throughout the country teaching and sharing poetry and stories with children and adults. She lives with her husband, David, and son, Eli, in Binghamton, New York, where she helped to found and create the Indoor Playground and the Book-bridge Bookstore in Vestal, New York.